For my family
—K.B.

Text copyright © 2005 by Kate Banks
Pictures copyright © 2005 by Georg Hallensleben
All rights reserved
Distributed in Canada by Douglas & McIntyre Publishing Group
Color separations by Chroma Graphics PTE Ltd.
Printed and bound in the United States of America by Berryville Graphics
Designed by Nancy Goldenberg
First edition, 2005
1 3 5 7 9 10 8 6 4 2

www.fsgkidsbooks.com

Library of Congress Cataloging-in-Publication Data
Banks, Kate, 1960–
    The great blue house / Kate Banks ; pictures by Georg Hallensleben.— 1st ed.
        p.   cm.
    Summary: When its owners leave, a summer house comes alive with the sounds of a
mouse nibbling crumbs in the fall, a cat taking shelter in the winter, and rain falling on the
roof in the spring.
    ISBN-13: 978-0-374-32769-9
    ISBN-10: 0-374-32769-6
    [1. Dwellings—Fiction.   2. Seasons—Fiction.]   I. Hallensleben, Georg, ill.   II. Title.

PZ7.B22594Gr 2005
[E]—dc22
                                                                        2003054886

The Great Blue House

KATE BANKS

Pictures by GEORG HALLENSLEBEN

Frances Foster Books

Farrar, Straus and Giroux • New York

It is summer at the great blue house.
The crickets are singing.
Clothes billow on the line.
The children crouch beside a stream chasing frogs.
Their voices rise into the air like dandelion puff.
Listen to them giggle and shout.

Inside, a pot bubbles over on the stove.
Water gurgles through the pipes.
At night the lights in the windows blink to the fireflies in the garden.

Then little by little the days grow shorter.
Dewdrops sparkle on the lawn.
Suitcases bang closed. Car doors slam shut.
"Goodbye, house," cry the children.

The gate is locked. The windows are sealed tight.
In the yard the grass lies flat.
All is quiet at the great blue house. Or is it?

In the kitchen a faucet drips.
A cupboard swings open.
A mouse is busy finishing off the last crumbs from summer.
Listen to him nibbling.

Outside, the leaves flutter and shake as they float to the ground.
Fall has come to the great blue house.
In a corner a spider spins a web in the last rays of day.
She watches the frost make designs on the windowpanes.
Listen to it buckle and crack.

Somewhere a latch gives way. Here comes a stray cat looking for mice.
She wanders through the house making mischief.
She pounces and knocks a candle to the floor.
Then she curls up in the woodbox close to the stove.
Listen to her sharpening her claws.

High in the house a rope swings gently back and forth.
A bird is hiding far from the cat.

The pipes freeze and the water stops dripping.
Snow falls lightly on the roof.
Winter has come to the great blue house.
The cat creeps cautiously out of doors.
She scuttles about, then returns to the woodbox.
Listen to her shaking the flakes from her fur.

The mouse is hiding in a closet.
Listen to him tugging on a pair of shoelaces.

Suddenly the cat's ears perk up.
Someone is knocking.
It's the rain come to wake up the garden.
Spring has come to the great blue house.

Crocuses push through the ground.
A snail thrusts its head out of its shell.
In the loft the bird is making a nest from sticks and a scrap of clothing.

There goes the cat up the stairs.
She pokes her head in each small corner.
Then she stretches out across the bed and settles into a secret dream.
Listen to her purring.

**The pipes thaw and water drips into the kitchen sink.
Overhead the bird sits patiently on her nest.
What is she waiting for?**

Off in the distance a dog barks.

At last a gate swings open. Windows are thrown up, doors stretched wide.

"Hello, house," cry the children, pulling out the fishing poles and oars.

Listen to them bang about.

The teakettle whistles and bare feet sound on the back stairs.

But what are those other noises?

Kittens are meowing.
Fledglings are chirping.
And a new baby cries.
Summer has returned to the great blue house.